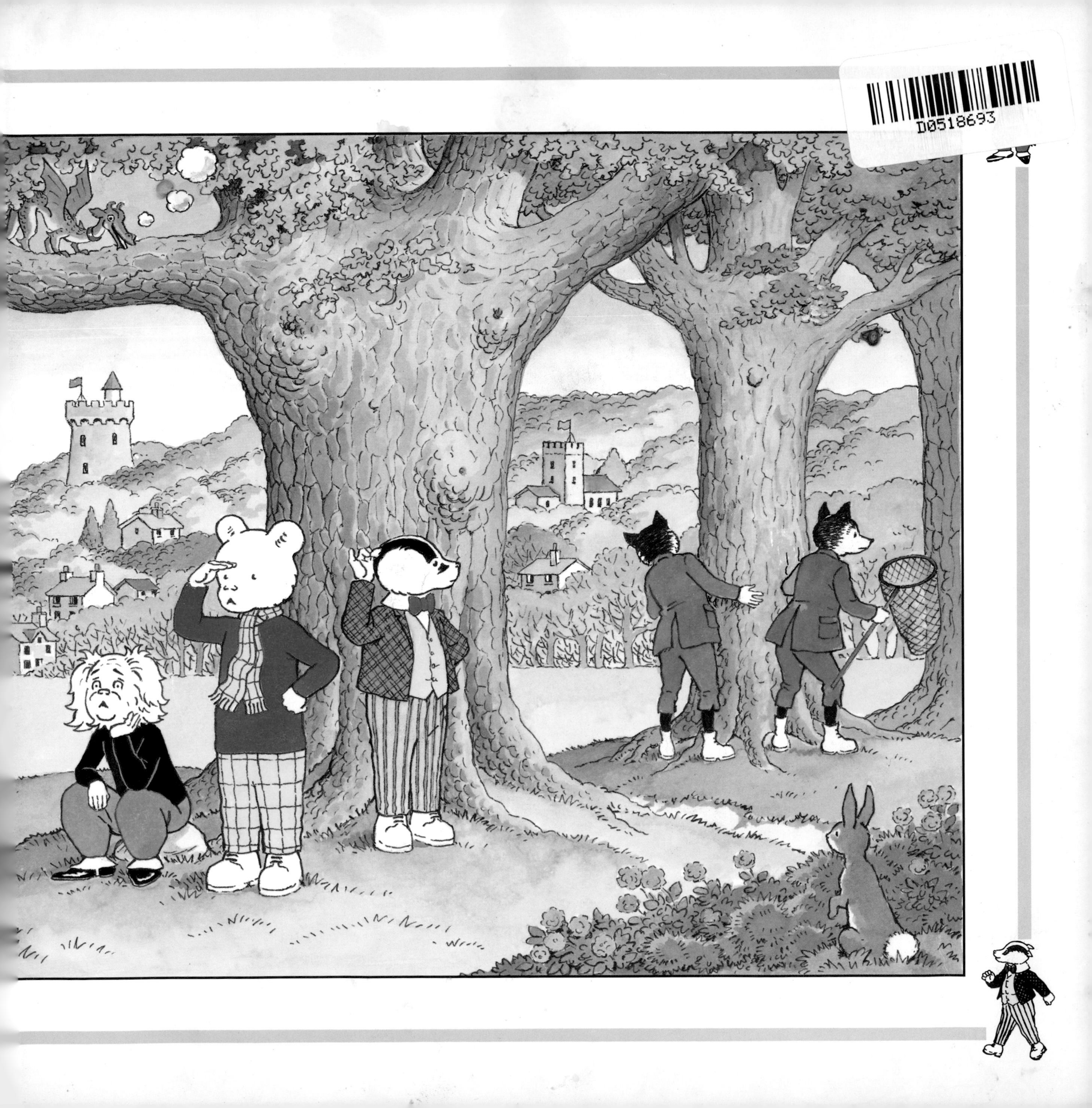

EXPRESS NEWSPAPERS plc, Ludgate House,
245 Blackfriars Road,
London SE1 9UX

Produced by Brainwaves Limited
5 Highwood Ridge, Hatch Warren, Basingstoke,
Hampshire RG22 4UU.

ISBN 0–85079–245–2

Printed and bound in Singapore

RUPERT
and the Lost Dragon

It's a lovely sunny day. Rupert and his pal, Bill Badger are off to see their friend Pong-Ping. Visiting him is always fun, because he has a very unusual pet. Instead of having a dog or cat, like most people, Pong-Ping has a dragon called Ming.

They reach his house and knock at the door. When Pong-Ping opens it he looks rather worried. "Whatever is wrong?" asks Rupert. "Oh dear! You won't believe what has happened," replies Pong-Ping. "Whatever shall I do?"

"We'll help you to find him," says Rupert. "Let's go and ask P.C. Growler at the police station." They set off towards Nutwood Village, but as they pass by the Chinese conjurer's pagoda, they see puffs of smoke coming from the windows.

"Look at that smoke" cries Pong-Ping. "Perhaps my dragon is inside." They knock at the door and are greeted by the Chinese conjurer's daughter, Tigerlily. As she opens the door wider, they see what is making all the smoke.

Saying goodbye to Tigerlily and her father, the three pals set off to see P.C. Growler. “He’s sure to be able to help,” says Bill. When they reach the police station, there is a big green box, with holes in it, standing on the desk.

“I’ve lost my pet dragon,” Pong-Ping starts to explain to the policeman. But, just then they hear noises coming from the box. “Perhaps someone has found Ming already,”cries Rupert, as P.C. Growler starts to open the box.

"Who else can help us?" wonders Pong-Ping. "I know," cries Rupert. "The Old Professor. He may even have a machine for finding lost things." The pals agree and set off towards the Old Professor's tower, which lies on the outskirts of Nutwood.

As they walk down the High Street, Bill gives a sudden cry. "Smoke!" he yells. "Look! In the toyshop window." They all rush to the toyshop window and there, sure enough, they can see little puffs of smoke. Could it be Ming?

The three disappointed friends continue on their way, but as they pass near the post box they hear a strange noise. "Listen!" says Rupert. "Perhaps Ming is hiding inside."

They stop and listen carefully. Rupert and his friends try to peep inside the big red post box, but it's too dark to see anything. "It doesn't sound like Ming," says Pong-Ping. "It sounds more like someone giggling." Then, Rupert takes a look behind the post box . . .

Rupert, Bill and Pong-Ping leave Nutwood Village and go towards the Old Professor's tower, where they are greeted by his little servant. "Come quickly," he says, "My master has something very special to show you."

When they see the Old Professor, Pong-Ping leaps with joy. It's because he can see a scaly tail peeping from beneath a cloth that the Old Professor is carrying. "It's Ming!" exclaims Pong-Ping, as the Old Professor removes the cloth.

Sadly, the pals decide to go back to Pong-Ping's house. Perhaps his pet dragon has found its own way home. Passing through the woods, Rupert stops and sniffs. "I'm sure that I can smell smoke," he says.

They all stop and sniff the air. "Yes, it's smoke all right," Bill agrees. "But where is it coming from?" They look all around and find that the smoke seems to be coming from underground. "What's making all this smoke?" asks Pong-Ping. "Could it be Ming, at last?" Suddenly, a trap door is flung open.

The three friends wave goodbye to the Autumn Elves and wish them better luck with their experiments. As they trudge back to Pong-Ping's house they're all feeling very miserable. "Perhaps I shall never see Ming again," sobs Pong-Ping sadly.

They search the house once more, but there's still no sign of the lost dragon. "I think I can hear something inside this big cauldron," says Rupert. Pong-Ping hurries to lift the lid and the three friends peer hopefully inside . . .